# Lucky the Rescued Puppy

# Lucky the Rescued Puppy

Holly Webb

Illustrated by Sophy Williams

**SCHOLASTIC INC.**

For Ethan and Harry

ISBN 978-0-545-47435-1

12 11 10 9 8 7 6 5 4 3        12 13 14 15 16 17/0

Printed in the U.S.A.                    40
First Scholastic printing, September 2012

# Chapter One

"I still think the blue leash was better," Adam said, staring down at Lucky's new leash with his arms folded and a sulky expression on his face.

"No, red looks so nice with his fur. If you hadn't spent all your allowance money on candy, you could have bought the new leash!" Georgia pointed out. "This is Lucky's first real walk. Do you want Mom to say we can't go because we're fighting? She will, you know!"

"Oh, all right . . ." Adam muttered. Then he grinned at his twin sister. "I don't think you're going to be able to get the leash on him, anyway!"

Lucky, Georgia and Adam's cocker spaniel puppy, was dancing around Georgia's feet, squeaking and yipping with excitement.

"Lucky, keep still!" Georgia giggled, trying to hook the leash on to his collar. "We won't ever get to go on the walk if you won't let me clip this on!"

"Are you two ready yet?" Mom came into the hallway. "Where are we going for this special walk?"

"The park!"

"The woods!"

Georgia and Adam spoke at the same time, and Mom sighed. "I think Adam's probably got the best idea this time, Georgie. The woods might be too tiring for Lucky on his first big walk. The paths are so narrow, and there's lots of scrambling over fallen trees and things. Let's get him used to something easier first."

Georgia sighed. "Okay. I bet he'll love the woods when he's bigger, though. Oooh!" She quickly clipped the leash on to Lucky's collar while the puppy was distracted looking at Mom. "There! Now we're ready!"

Lucky pulled excitedly at the new leash, twirling himself around Georgia's ankles. He had been on a leash before, for his trips to the vet and the puppy parties he'd been to, to get used to other dogs, but it was still very exciting. He could feel that Georgia and Adam were excited about something, too, and he couldn't stop jumping up and down.

Adam and Georgia had gotten Lucky two months before, as a joint ninth birthday present. They had been trying to persuade their parents to get a dog forever, and Mom and Dad had finally decided that they were old enough. Luckily, Georgia and Adam had agreed that they would really love a spaniel. One of their friends at school, Max, had a gorgeous black cocker spaniel named Jet, and they both loved to play with him when Max's mom brought him to pick up Max after school.

Georgia and Adam's mom had asked where Jet had come from, and Max's mom had given her the name of the cocker spaniel breeder. She told them the puppies were all well looked after and used to children. But when Georgia and Adam's mom called the breeder, there was only one ten-week-old puppy left, and a new litter wasn't expected for a long time. So the whole family had driven right over to see him.

At first, all they could see was the puppy's mom, lying on a fluffy blanket. She was the most beautiful golden and white spaniel, with the longest, silkiest ears they'd ever seen.

"Oh, wow . . ." Georgia breathed. "Can we pet her?"

Lara, the breeder, nodded. "Just gently, though. You have to be careful with mother dogs when they've got their puppies with them."

Adam frowned. "But she doesn't— I can't see a puppy!"

Georgia grabbed his hand. "Look!" she said in an excited whisper. "I just saw him—he's fast asleep, snuggled up right next to her. He's adorable!"

Adam leaned over. "I thought that

was his mom's tail," he admitted. "He's really cute. And tiny!"

Lara laughed. "You should have seen him when he was born. He isn't really that small—I actually think his mom's sitting on him."

Georgia knelt down to get a closer look. "Yes, she is. Doesn't he mind?"

"No, he's all warm and cozy. He likes

being the only pup left, since it means he gets all the attention from his mom and from all of us. He's going to want a lot of cuddling if you take him home."

Adam and Georgia exchanged grins. That sounded perfect.

Just then, the little dog sighed, yawned, and opened his eyes. He looked over at his mother and wriggled his bottom indignantly to tell her to get off. Then he heaved himself up and peered around, his tail wagging shyly. Who were all these people staring at him?

"Oh, he's so beautiful. . . ." Georgia whispered, then turned to her mom and dad. "Look at him, isn't he perfect?"

He really was like a perfect mini version of his mom, curly ears and all.

He was golden and white, with pretty white patches on his back and a scatter of sweet brownish-gold spots around his shiny black nose. His eyes were nearly black, too, and very bright and curious looking, topped off with long whiskery eyebrows that made him look like a little old man.

Everyone agreed that he was the perfect puppy, and Lara said that they could come back and take him home the very next day. It was a few weeks before Georgia and Adam's birthday, but they didn't mind getting their present early. The following day, they carefully carried the puppy out of Lara's house to put him into the new pet carrier in the back of the car. Georgia pointed out that they were lucky to have him at all. If they had waited any longer, there might not have been any puppies left.

"And he's lucky to have us, too," Adam said. "I bet he wouldn't have liked anybody else as much. Oof!" He laughed and wiped off a smear of saliva, as the puppy gave him a wet dog kiss across his chin.

"That's what we should call him!"

Georgia said suddenly. "Lucky! It's exactly right!"

Soon, Adam and Georgia couldn't imagine not having Lucky. He was very friendly, and played endless games of chase and fetch with them in the yard. He loved running so much that he'd bound up and down, and then just suddenly flop down on the grass and fall asleep, absolutely worn out. Georgia called it his "off button." It made her burst out laughing every time.

But although Lucky loved running around the yard, Adam and Georgia had learned that cocker spaniels shouldn't really go on actual walks until they were about four or five months old. Adam had read it in the book they'd bought, and on a special cocker spaniel website. Georgia hadn't believed him at first.

"Why not?" she'd demanded.

Adam had shrugged. "It says they love long walks when they're older—*lots* of long walks—but you shouldn't wear them out too much when they're little. Just exercise in the yard."

Now that they had Lucky, Georgia could understand why both the website and the book had suggested that. Lucky was still quite a small dog, but he was getting heavy. If they'd gone on a long walk and he'd switched off like he did when they were playing, he'd be a real armful to carry all the way home. But now that he was almost five months old, he wasn't getting nearly as tired. Mom and Dad agreed that he was ready for a real walk, just as long as they were careful not to go too far.

Luckily, the park was close enough that they'd be able to carry the puppy home if he did get really worn out.

Adam opened the front door, and Lucky sniffed the air outside. The front yard smelled different than the back— more cars, and there was definitely a cat hanging around somewhere. He looked up at Georgia hopefully. Were they going out?

She laughed at his eager little face. "Come on!"

Adam ran down the path to open the gate, and Lucky gave an excited squeak.

"Try and remember not to let him pull!" Mom called as she locked the front door and hurried after them. Georgia and Adam had started going to puppy obedience classes soon after they brought Lucky home. They'd spent a lot of time working on walking to heel, but Lucky was so excited at going somewhere new that there wasn't much chance of him doing that now.

"Oh, yes." Georgia quickly grabbed a dog treat out of her pocket and held it in front of Lucky's nose, moving it back so that he was standing by the side of her leg, as she'd practiced in the puppy obedience classes. Then she walked on down the path and gave Lucky the treat as he trotted nicely alongside her.

"We can run with him in the park, though, can't we?" Adam asked Mom.

"I don't mean we'll let him off the leash—I know he's not old enough for that. But can we run fast with him?"

"Of course you can!" Mom smiled. "It's just best to try and keep him under control on the way there. Of course, we can't expect Lucky to act perfectly, since it's all so different from our yard at home."

But Lucky had stopped wanting to dance around anyway. He was much too busy for that. When he'd gone out before, to puppy training and trips in the car to visit friends, he'd always been carried. There was so much more to see down at nose level now! To see and thoroughly sniff.

Georgia giggled as they stopped at the seventh lamppost—still on their street. "You know, if we want to be back by dinnertime, I'm not sure we're going to make it to the park!"

# Chapter Two

They only made it just inside the park on that first walk before Lucky started to drag on his leash and look up hopefully, wanting to be picked up. Georgia and Adam took turns carrying the weary puppy home.

But over the next few weeks, a short walk every day soon stretched to two short walks, and then a quick run around the block before breakfast and a real walk after school, in the park or the woods. By the time Georgia and Adam went on summer vacation, walks were his absolute favorite thing.

They celebrated the beginning of break by taking a picnic lunch with them to the woods. It was a beautiful, hot day, perfect for a long expedition. Mom took a folding chair, so she could sit down with a book while Georgia, Adam, and Lucky raced around the woods, shouting and calling and playing hide-and-seek among the tree roots.

Lucky adored the woods. They were full of amazing smells, good places to dig, and sticks that Georgia and Adam could throw for him to chase. He had an extending leash now, since no one was sure about letting him run free just yet. But the absolute best thing about the woods was that they were full of squirrels. Lucky loved squirrels. They were fast, they smelled interesting, and they bounced up and down when they scampered along. He was desperate to catch one. He'd never gotten anywhere near one, but he wasn't giving up hope. And there was a squirrel now. . . .

Adam raced behind Lucky, laughing as the puppy pulled the leash out to its full length and galloped down the path, ears flapping as if he was about to take off. The squirrel was a plump, bushy-tailed one, and it wasn't scared. It seemed to keep looking back to see how close the puppy was getting.

"Adam!" Georgia yelled worriedly.

"Don't let him catch it! He'll hurt it! Or it might scratch him!"

But Adam was too far away to hear —or he just wasn't listening, Georgia thought, annoyed, as she dashed after them. She really didn't want Lucky to hurt the squirrel.

But when she caught up with Adam and Lucky, she saw that she shouldn't have worried. Adam was leaning against a tree, panting, and Lucky was jumping up and down and scrabbling at the trunk, whimpering.

The squirrel was sitting on a branch halfway up, squeaking and chittering as though it was scolding Lucky.

"Didn't you hear me yelling?" Georgia demanded. "What do you think he'd do if he caught it?"

Adam shook his head and shrugged. "No idea! I don't think he knows, either. Calm down, Georgie! He's never going to get one."

Lucky ignored them, staring hopefully up at the squirrel as it danced up and down on its branch. Unfortunately for him, it didn't look like it was going to fall off.

By the time they trailed back to the clearing where Mom was sitting, they were all really hungry. They had brought Lucky's dog food with them, and a bottle of water and his bowl, so he could have a picnic, too. He wolfed down the kibble in about two seconds, and then stood staring at Adam's tuna sandwich as if he were starved.

Georgia giggled. "You should learn to like vegetables, Adam. He never wants *my* sandwiches."

Adam shuddered. "Yuck."

Mom slipped her cardigan off her shoulders, enjoying the sun. "Just think, this time next week we'll be on vacation at the beach!"

Georgia opened her chips and sneakily fed a very small one to Lucky. He wasn't really supposed to have them, but she couldn't resist those big, hopeful dark eyes.

"We've never been on vacation with a dog before," Adam said happily, stretching himself out on the blanket.

"We'll be by the ocean, right?" Georgia asked. She already knew they would be—she'd seen the photos in the vacation rental brochure—but she liked to hear her mom say it.

Mom smiled over at her. "Absolutely next to it, Georgie. A little cottage right at the top of a cliff."

"And we'll be allowed to take Lucky for walks, all by ourselves?" Adam pushed himself up on his elbows.

"As long as you're very, very careful and responsible." Mom and Dad had discussed this with them when they'd first booked the cottage. It was in a conservation area where there were no roads—just a little track that led up to the cottage.

Adam and Georgia nodded. They would be super-careful. They lived in a busy town, close to a main road that they had to cross in order to get anywhere, so Mom and Dad weren't happy about letting them take Lucky out on their own at home. That was why they had looked for a vacation home situated in a quiet place. Cliff Cottage wasn't far from a pretty seaside town called Woolbridge, but it was all on its own on a cliff, surrounded by trails. It was going to be wonderful.

"I'm going to start packing when we get home," Georgia said dreamily. "We'll have to remember to pack all of Lucky's things, too. I wonder if there's a pet store in Woolbridge."

Adam smirked. "So you can buy him another fancy collar?" Then he rolled out of the way as Georgia aimed a smack at him.

Lucky gave a little warning bark.

He didn't like it when they squabbled. He didn't understand that they were just joking around, even though Georgia had tried telling him it was just what twins did. It seemed to him that they were really angry with each other. He looked from Georgia to Adam and back again, his eyes worried, and whined sadly.

"Sorry, Lucky." Georgia wriggled over to him and rubbed his ears and scratched his silky domed spaniel forehead. "It's okay. We didn't mean it."

Lucky flopped down, head on paws, with a small sigh of relief. His eyes were closing, and within seconds he was asleep in the sun.

# Chapter Three

"I wish Lucky could sit in the backseat with us," said Georgia several days later as she gently placed the puppy in his travel crate behind the seats. She caught Dad's eye and sighed. "Oh, it's all right, Dad. I know he can't. But it's just such a long trip! He's going to be miserable stuck in that crate. And it would be so nice to have him to cuddle on the way."

Dad shook his head. "Until he starts jumping around and being silly, and distracting me and Mom when we're driving. Don't worry. We'll stop for a bathroom break halfway there, and we'll let Lucky out and you can take him to stretch his legs. He'll probably go to sleep, since we put his favorite blanket in the crate for him."

"I hope so," Georgia said, patting Lucky gently and rubbing his ears before she closed the door of the crate. "See you soon, sweetheart."

"You get in, Georgia. I'll go and see what's keeping your mom and Adam."

But Adam was already stomping down the path, lugging his bag and looking grumpy. Mom followed along behind, shaking her head.

"He'd repacked everything!" she told Dad. "And taken out half his clothes! It's a good thing I checked. He had a skateboard in there instead!"

Dad blinked. "But I already packed his skateboard—it's right next to Lucky's travel crate."

Mom rolled her eyes. "Apparently he needs two."

"Wow. Oh, wow . . ." Georgia breathed. She was standing in front of the cottage with Lucky in her arms, staring out at the sea. He hadn't minded the car ride that much—he'd slept most of the time, like she had hoped. But he was definitely glad to be out of his crate.

They'd only just arrived, and Georgia and Adam had piled out of the car with Lucky to go and look around.

"It's beautiful," Georgia murmured.

The sun was shining, and it had turned the water to silver, as though a sparkling pathway was stretched across the sea, calling them down to the beach.

"It really is right next to the ocean," Adam said, grinning. He turned around to look at the cottage behind them, a small, white building, very low to the ground, as if it was trying to hide from the winds that swept across the cliff top. "And there's the path down to the beach, look!" He pointed to a little path, half natural, but with steps carved into it here and there to make the steep climb to the sand easier.

"Can we go down . . . ?" Georgia started to say, but Mom was waving to them.

"Come and help unpack. It won't take long, and then we can all head to the beach."

Georgia sighed and headed back to the car to get her backpack. Lucky made a little whining noise, twisting in her arms to look at the glittering water. He wanted to go closer. He'd never seen anything like it before. Georgia hugged him tight. "I know, Lucky. I want to go and play down there, too. Soon, I promise."

She dashed inside, chasing after Adam, who was already stomping up the stairs. He flung open the bedroom door that Mom had pointed out, and yelled, "I get the top bunk!"

"Hey, not fair!" Georgia moaned from the doorway. Lucky wriggled out of her arms and went to explore. "Why do you get the top one? Can't we swap halfway through the trip?"

Adam climbed up the ladder to throw his bag on the bed and stared down at her smugly. "Nope. I called it. Get used to it, Georgie."

Georgia stamped her foot angrily, and Lucky, who was sniffing around under the bunk bed, backed farther underneath it, tucking his tail between his legs. They were fighting again. He hated it when they did that. Quietly, he sneaked along under the bed, making for the bedroom door. Then he bolted out as Georgia snapped at Adam, and stood shivering on the landing. He wanted to get away from the loud, scary voices.

Georgia and Adam's mom had been looking around, checking out the different rooms and starting to put things away. She'd opened the door of the large hall closet at the top of the stairs that contained the heating system, thinking to herself how useful it would be for drying off beach towels. Then she'd closed it again, but she didn't see that it had swung open a little as she walked away, and now Lucky nosed his way inside. It was warm and dark and safe next to the hot water tank, and no one was shouting in here. He curled up on an old towel that the last family must have left behind, and waited for his heart to stop thumping anxiously.

Back in the bedroom, Georgia suddenly stopped arguing and smiled as a thought occurred to her. "All right. You can have the top bunk. I don't mind."

"What?" Adam glared at her suspiciously. "For the whole time we're here?"

Georgia smiled even wider. "Yes. The whole time."

Adam nodded slowly. "Okay."

Georgia sat down on the bottom bunk and patted it happily. "Lucky won't be able to get up the ladder, you know. So I get him on my bed for the whole time."

At home, Lucky slept on either Georgia's bed or Adam's, depending on how he felt. Sometimes he switched in the middle of the night, but he was usually curled up on Georgia's toes when she woke up in the morning.

Adam scowled. "Hey, that's not fair!"

"You wanted the top bunk," Georgia sang triumphantly. "Now you've got it!"

Adam slumped down next to her. "Huh. Cheater."

"Nope, just smarter than you. Hey, where *is* Lucky?" Georgia sat up, looking around worriedly. "He was exploring a minute ago. Oh, no—he hates when we fight."

Adam jumped up off the bed. "What if he ran outside? He has no clue where he's going around here."

They raced out of the bedroom, calling worriedly. "Lucky! Here, Lucky! Where are you, boy?"

"Did you lose him?" Mom popped her head out of her bedroom, looking anxious. "Oh, you two! I heard you fighting—did you upset him?"

Dad came up the stairs. "I've been unloading the car and I haven't seen him come outside. He must be in the cottage somewhere. You really need to behave better around him, both of you. It's part of being good dog owners—you have to be careful not to frighten your puppy."

"Sorry, Dad," Adam and Georgia murmured, both looking guilty.

"He couldn't have gone far," said Dad. "Come on. I'll check downstairs and you two have another look up here."

"Maybe he's under the bed!" Adam dashed back into their room.

Georgia looked along the landing, wondering where she would hide if she were a frightened little puppy. Probably somewhere dark and cozy. Adam's guess that Lucky was under the bed made sense. . . . Then she spotted the hall closet door, still slightly open, and padded quietly over to it. She swung the door open gently and crouched down to peer inside.

Lucky stared back at Georgia, his eyes round and watchful, and thumped his tail slowly on the towel.

"Hey, Lucky," Georgia whispered sadly, looking at his worried little face. "We scared you, didn't we? Come on out, sweetie, we won't fight anymore."

Adam appeared behind her, and Georgia glanced up warningly, her finger to her lips. Adam nodded. "It's okay, Lucky," he whispered. "We'll be nice."

Lucky stood up and nosed at Georgia's hands lovingly. She picked him up, and Adam petted his ears gently.

"I'm really sorry, Lucky. Adam, we can't fight while we're here, okay?" Georgia looked at him seriously. "Or we have to try not to, anyway. We can't risk upsetting Lucky and having him run off to a strange place."

Adam nodded. "Vacation truce." He grinned. "Mom and Dad will be happy. Their quietest vacation ever!"

After the world's fastest lunch—Adam and Georgia both claimed they weren't hungry, but Mom refused to believe them—they finally got to go down to the beach to explore with Lucky. It was amazing. Because the beach wasn't really close to the town, there was hardly anybody there—just one family building a sand castle, and a group of older boys swimming over at one end.

"There's a bigger beach just a little farther along the coast, by Woolbridge, with an ice cream stand and a pier," Mom explained. "But you aren't allowed to take dogs onto Woolbridge Beach in the summer."

"I don't mind." Georgia gazed at the brown sand, which was striped with pebbles and framed by the tall, reddish-brown cliffs. "It's lovely here. Just us and the ocean. Do you think we could let Lucky off the leash? He'd have to go all the way back up the path to get lost."

Dad nodded. "As long as we keep an eye on him."

Lucky barked excitedly as Georgia unclipped his leash. He wasn't used to being allowed to run off wherever he liked, and at first he simply raced up and down the sand, barking and jumping and chasing his tail.

Then he spotted an interesting pile of smelly seaweed that had been washed up and left on the beach by the tide. Georgia could see a line of it, all the way along the sand—seaweed, and shells, and even a piece of beautiful emerald green sea glass that she slipped into her pocket as a souvenir.

Adam was already splashing around in the ocean, but Georgia decided she needed a little more time in the sun before taking a dip in the chilly water. She wondered if it might be too cold for Lucky, too. But Sam, their obedience class teacher, had told them spaniels usually loved water.

Lucky started to dig furiously, loving the way the sand spurted up between his paws. It was much quicker to dig here than in the flower beds at home. But it did go everywhere. He stopped mid-hole to shake the sand out of his whiskers, and let out an enormous sneeze. Next he scrabbled a big pile of seaweed into his hole and covered it back up, scooting the sand back through his paws. Then he sat down on it happily, looking very proud of himself.

Georgia watched him, laughing. "Shall we go and see the water now?" she asked him. "Look, Adam's swimming in it."

Lucky stood up and followed her down to the water's edge, where Adam was hopping in and out of the wavelets, whistling through his teeth at how cold it was.

Lucky watched interestedly, his tail wagging. He'd never seen so much water, and it moved! He backed away thoughtfully as the bubbly surf crept toward him, and then followed it back again, fascinated.

"Oh, look, Adam, he loves it!" Georgia giggled.

The puppy crouched down, his paws stretched out in front of him, wondering if he could catch this stuff. This time, when the creamy water began to draw back from his paws, he jumped after it, splashing himself and Georgia with freezing cold water.

Georgia laughed, and Lucky shook

himself in surprise. He hadn't expected that to happen. But he liked it!

When the next wave came, he didn't try to catch the water, he just jumped in and out of it, shaking his soaked ears and whining excitedly. Chasing the waves was almost as much fun as chasing squirrels!

# Chapter Four

On that first afternoon of their vacation, Georgia and Adam had been so eager to get down to the beach that they'd hardly taken anything with them. But the next morning, the first full day in Woolbridge, they took everything. Beach toys, towels, snacks, a big blanket, and Adam's enormous inflatable alligator. They struggled down the path, laden with all they could possibly need, and Mom and Dad followed them with folding chairs and the picnic.

It was another beautiful, sunny day, and Mom insisted on covering them with sunblock as soon as they'd set up a base camp next to a large rock. She looked doubtfully at Lucky. "I suppose he'll be all right. But if he starts to look hot, bring him back over here and he can lie down in the shade of the rocks."

"Okay, but he'll probably just splash in the water like he did yesterday," Georgia pointed out. "That'll keep him nice and cool."

Lucky was already running up and down the water's edge, barking excitedly at seagulls, who shrieked back. One of them settled down to float on the greenish water, not very far out, and glared at him.

Lucky splashed into the ocean, far enough that it came halfway up his short legs, and barked a challenge. But the seagull only bobbed up and down, and kept on staring. Lucky took a few more steps in, shivering a little as the water came up to his chest.

Georgia had been sitting rubbing sunblock into her arms and watching Adam, who was kicking a ball around farther up the beach. But now she suddenly noticed that Lucky was in the water. She raced down to the edge of the ocean, but Dad was there already.

"It's okay, Georgie. Lots of dogs are good swimmers. We shouldn't let him go out too far, but don't scare him now. We don't want him to think the water's something to be afraid of."

Georgia frowned. Actually, she thought maybe they did. What if Lucky got swept away by a big wave? And that seagull looked like it wanted puppy for breakfast. It was staring at Lucky evilly with its tiny yellow eyes.

Lucky looked around, pleased to see Georgia so close, and then took another step forward. Strangely, though, his paws didn't seem to find any ground to step on, and all of a sudden he was swimming, dog-paddling as though he'd been doing it forever. Surprised at himself, he paddled around in a little circle, almost forgetting about the seagull.

"He's swimming! He's swimming!" Georgia yelled. "Lucky can swim! Dad, look!"

The seagull flapped its powerful wings and fluttered away with loud, frightened squawks, and Lucky barked after it.

"Sorry, Lucky!" Georgia splashed into the water. "I forgot you were chasing him. You're such a smart boy! How did you learn to swim? Come on!" She dog-paddled along with him, even though she was in such shallow water that her knees kept hitting the sand. "Do you think he can swim a little farther out, Dad?" she called.

Dad shook his head. "Maybe not yet —he might get tired quickly, like he

did with walks at first. He's never done
it before, remember. Just splash around
in the shallow water with him."

Adam came running down the beach
to join in. They spent the next hour
swimming out to sea and then back to
the beach and letting the little waves
carry them up onto the sand, while
Lucky swam and splashed and barked
delightedly around them.

They were worn out by lunchtime, so much so that Lucky went to sleep in the shade of the big rock after he'd eaten his food and had a big drink of water. Adam and Georgia lazed around reading while their sandwiches digested—Mom said they had to wait for a while before going back in the water.

"It's been ages since lunch," Adam moaned. "Can we go swimming again?"

"It's only been about ten minutes!" Mom laughed, and Adam sighed.

"All right. I'm going to blow up my alligator." He lay down on the blanket and started to puff fiercely, till the alligator was longer than he was. "Now is it swimming time?"

Mom looked at her watch. "Yes, I guess so. Oh, Lucky!"

Lucky had just woken up and found an enormous green thing next to Adam, which definitely hadn't been there when he went to sleep. He raced over and barked at it wildly, circling around it, kicking sand at everybody.

"Ugh! Stop him!" Mom coughed, and Adam snatched the alligator up above his head, while Georgia grabbed Lucky.

"Lucky, stop, shhh! It's not a real one, silly. It's for swimming. Come on, Adam, let's show him. The water will wash the sand off us, too." She carried the squirming puppy down to the water's edge, and Adam launched the alligator into the waves.

"We'll have to be careful that Lucky doesn't burst it with his claws," he said, holding the alligator steady.

Georgia leaped onboard and lay down. "You can pull us," she suggested, holding on to the side. "Come on, Lucky." She held out an arm, expecting the puppy to swim toward it, but instead he splashed into the water, paddled out to her, then scrambled up onto her back.

"You're a raft!" Adam yelled, and Georgia giggled, trying not to wriggle too much and tip Lucky off. His claws tickled.

They swam up and down, taking turns on the alligator, and then pulled it up onto the beach and lay there on the sand, letting the tiny waves wash over their toes.

The sun was so hot, even when they were half in the water, that Georgia almost fell asleep. She was just wondering how it was that the water seemed as warm as a bath now, when it had been freezing when she first dipped her toes in that morning, when Adam suddenly sat up and yelled, "Look! The alligator!"

She turned over and sat up. "What's the matter?"

"I wasn't watching. The tide came in," Adam groaned. "The waves have taken it out. I'll have to swim after it."

Georgia stood up. "I can't even see it. Oh, no! Adam, you can't swim all the way out there."

The alligator was only a little green speck, about a hundred feet from the shore. They'd be far out of their depth.

"Dad!" Adam called. But their dad still had all his clothes on, and even though he was heading over toward them, and Mom was standing up, looking worried, neither of them looked like they were about to dive into the ocean.

"Dad, can I swim out and get the alligator?" Adam begged. But Dad shook his head.

"I'm really sorry, Adam. It's drifted too far. You promised not to go out of your depth, remember? Maybe someone in a boat will come past and pick it up for us."

Adam and Georgia looked hopefully out to sea, but there were no boats around to go alligator hunting, and the inflatable toy was bobbing farther and farther away.

Then Adam grabbed Georgia's arm and pointed. A little golden head was suddenly bobbing through the dark green water. Lucky could see the inflatable alligator, and he knew that Adam wanted it back. He wasn't quite sure why Adam wasn't going to get it himself, but he knew he could help.

"Lucky, no!" Georgia gasped. But Lucky was already way out into the sea, swimming along happily.

"He's too far out," Georgia murmured

worriedly. "What if he gets caught in a current and swept right out to sea?"

Adam nodded. "Let's swim as far as we can—then we can help him back."

They swam as fast as they could to where their toes were only just touching the bottom. Mom and Dad were watching carefully. Although Georgia and Adam had promised they wouldn't go out of their depth, secretly Georgia knew that if Lucky started sinking, she'd follow him right out into the deep water. And she was sure Adam would do the same.

But they didn't need to. Slowly but surely, the alligator was bobbing back toward them, Lucky's sharp teeth gripping the white tow rope.

"You're amazing, Lucky! You rescued my alligator!" Adam grabbed the rope, too, and Georgia hugged Lucky, who snuggled wearily into her shoulder. It had been a long swim, and his legs were very tired. But he had done it! Georgia and Adam were happy, he could tell.

"Georgie, you get up on the alligator with him, and I'll pull you along," Adam suggested.

Georgia nodded and heaved herself up onto the inflatable, carefully keeping Lucky's claws away from the plastic. Adam towed them back in, with Georgia proudly holding Lucky in front of her.

Mom and Dad were waiting for them on the beach, smiling with relief.

"I can't believe what a good swimmer he is!" Mom said, stroking Lucky's soaking-wet ears.

"He's a champion," Adam said proudly. "We'd have lost my alligator for sure if it wasn't for Lucky."

Georgia turned over in bed and yawned, and then giggled as a damp nose was pressed into her ear. "Hello, Lucky! Is it time to get up?" She wriggled up in bed and pulled open the curtains to look out of the little window right next to the bunks.

"Oh!" Georgie wrinkled her nose disappointedly. The sparkling blue water from the day before had disappeared. The sky was cloudy and the sea had settled to a dull grayish brown—it didn't look like a day for sunbathing or swimming at all.

"Oh, well," Georgie murmured. "Never mind, Lucky. Maybe we can go exploring along the cliffs instead."

She got out of bed and threw on jeans and a T-shirt. She could already hear Mom and Dad moving around downstairs, and she thought she could smell toast. Lucky would need to go out into the tiny yard behind the cottage to do his business.

"Wake up, Adam," she called, tickling the foot that was dangling down over the edge of the top bunk as she went past.

Adam growled something, but his covers shifted, so she knew he was at least partly awake.

"Let's go and explore the cliffs this morning," Georgia suggested a few minutes later as she sat down at the table for breakfast. Lucky was already sitting hopefully by her foot, waiting for toast crusts.

But Adam shook his head grumpily.

"No! I really want to go down to the beach at Woolbridge. You said we could, Dad! They've got rides on the pier there and everything. I was talking to those boys we saw on the beach on our first day, and they said it's awesome there."

Georgia frowned. "But we wouldn't be able to take Lucky! Woolbridge Beach doesn't allow dogs in the summer, Mom said."

"Anyway, it's not such nice weather today," Mom put in. "It feels more like a day for walking along the cliffs than going to the beach. We'll do that another day, Adam."

Adam muttered something under his breath, but Mom managed to distract him by passing him chocolate spread for his toast, which was a special treat.

After breakfast, they set off along the path that led from the cottage, winding through the bracken and brambles along the top of the cliff. Lucky danced ahead, tugging on his extending leash, and winding himself in and out of the brambles as he investigated all the interesting sandy holes.

"Let's take him off the leash," Georgia suggested after she had unwound him from the bramble bushes for the third time. "There's no one else up here."

But before Dad could answer, Lucky uttered a sharp little woof and looked at her excitedly.

"What is it?" she asked, and then she gasped. "Oh, look! A rabbit!"

A small sandy brown rabbit was

peering back at them from the middle of a bramble bush. It looked terrified.

"Poor thing!" Georgia whispered. "It's so scared. Lucky, don't chase it!" But Lucky was already darting forward, the cord of his leash getting longer as he raced after the rabbit, which turned tail and dived down a nearby hole.

"Oh, Lucky!" Georgia tried to pull him back, but he had his nose in the hole and was barking frantically. He'd been within a few feet of a real rabbit, and now it had disappeared! He could smell it still, but he couldn't see it. He dug and scrabbled, but he couldn't get any farther in—the hole was too narrow. Eventually, he gave up and slunk sadly back to Georgia. For some reason she seemed upset, but he had no idea why.

"That rabbit was terrified! You shouldn't have chased it, Lucky!"

Adam snorted. "Come on, Georgie, he's a dog! That's what dogs do! Spaniels were bred for hunting."

"But Lucky's a pet, not a hunting dog! What if he gets to like hunting things and starts chasing cats?"

Georgia snapped back. "Then he'd be in real trouble. Imagine what Mrs. Winter next door would do if he chased Percy!" Percy was Mrs. Winter's enormous fluffy Persian cat. Georgia sighed, looking down at Lucky, who was watching her with confused eyes and slowly wagging his tail. "Oh, it isn't your fault, Lucky. I'm not really angry. It was such a cute rabbit, that's all."

"Anyway, that answers the question about letting him off the leash," Dad pointed out. "Have you noticed how close we are to the edge of the cliff?" He crouched down, pushing aside some clumps of yellow flowers to show the animal holes dotted around between them—and the little sandy slope trailing down to the edge. "If a rabbit popped up in front of Lucky and ducked into one of those holes there, he'd be over the side of the cliff before you could even call his name."

Georgia shuddered. "I guess you're right. Okay, we'll keep the leash on."

Lucky wandered ahead, sniffing hopefully for more rabbits, but they all seemed to have hidden themselves away. For the rest of the walk he had to make do with leaping at the butterflies. There were lots of tiny little blue ones, which kept recklessly flying around his nose.

# Chapter Five

The next couple of days were sunny again, and the family spent them on the beach. Lucky and the children were in and out of the water most of the time, since it was so hot that it was the only way to cool down.

The group of boys who'd been on the beach before were back again on Wednesday, playing soccer, and Adam watched them hopefully for a while before the ball happened to come past him. He kicked it back expertly, and they invited him to come and join in. Georgia didn't mind being left on her own with Lucky and Mom and Dad. It was too hot for soccer, and it was fun reading her book with Lucky snoozing next to her in the sun.

"Mom! Dad! Josh and Liam's dad's taking them to Woolbridge Beach this afternoon, and they asked if I want to go, too. Can I? And can I take my allowance money for the rides?"

Dad got up and went to talk to Josh and Liam's dad.

"What about you, Georgia?" Mom asked. "Dad and I could take you if you wanted to go over to Woolbridge."

Georgia looked thoughtful, but then she shook her head. "Actually, I'd rather stay here, Mom." She didn't love rides, and she was really enjoying spending her vacation time with Lucky.

Adam went off with the other boys after their picnic lunch, and Georgia set off on a long walk up the beach with Lucky. She hunted for shells and sea glass, and Lucky found a dead fish. He was quite upset when Georgia threw it back into the water and wouldn't let him fetch it. It had smelled delicious.

On Thursday morning, Georgia and Adam were hoping to go to the beach again, but Mom pointed out that they really needed to go and do some grocery shopping.

"Do we have to come?" Adam groaned.

"Well, you can't go to the beach by yourselves." Mom shook her head. "Dad or I need to be there if you're going in the water."

"We could just stay out of the water," Georgia suggested. But then she shook her head. "Actually, I don't see how we'd explain to Lucky that he couldn't go swimming. It probably isn't a very good idea."

"What about a walk, though?" Adam asked. "You did say before we came that we'd be allowed to go out on our own, and we haven't yet."

"Yes, and Lucky really needs a walk, too," Georgia added, exchanging an excited glance with Adam.

Mom and Dad looked thoughtfully at each other. "I suppose you could," Dad said slowly. "We won't be more than a couple of hours. As long as you take one of our cell phones, and you promise not to do anything foolish."

"Awesome!" Adam cheered, and Georgia reached under the table to pet Lucky. She could hardly wait to take their puppy out on their own for the first time ever.

After breakfast, Adam tucked Mom's cell phone safely away in the pocket of his shorts, and he and Georgia filled a little bag with sunblock, snacks, dog treats, water, and Lucky's special folding dog bowl. It was so hot that he was bound to need a drink.

It felt like a real adventure, setting off

on their own with Lucky, and they were determined to make it a really long walk.

"We could go all the way around the top of the bay," Adam suggested as he hurried along holding Lucky's leash. "The cliffs farther over toward Woolbridge looked really interesting from the beach. There might be caves and things in them. And we could look for fossils!"

But by the time they'd fought their way through the brambles as far as they'd gone on that first cliff-top walk, Georgia and Adam were so hot they decided to stop for a break. Georgia filled up Lucky's bowl, and he drank greedily. He'd walked more than twice as far as Georgia and Adam, since he kept running backward and forward. He lay there in the cool shade of the bracken, occasionally snapping lazily at flies as they buzzed past. Adam sat on the leash, just in case, but it didn't look like Lucky wanted to run off, anyway.

"My turn to take Lucky now," Georgia said as she packed his bowl away in the bag and got up. "You can carry the bag."

Adam scowled. "Why should you always get to hold his leash? I get him for this walk. You got him all yesterday afternoon!"

"What? For the whole walk? That isn't fair!" Georgia yelled. "I only had him yesterday because you wanted to go off to Woolbridge! You didn't care about Lucky then, did you?"

Lucky looked up and whined worriedly.

"Oh, it's okay, Lucky . . . don't be scared." She turned to her brother. "Now look!" she hissed. "You're upsetting Lucky!"

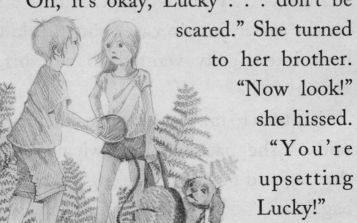

"I'm not the one arguing!" Adam spat back in a whisper. "Just let me hold the leash! This walk was my idea, remember?!"

"No! It's my turn!"

Lucky whined again, but they weren't listening. He backed away, the leash pulling out behind him, his tail held close against his legs. He didn't want to be near them when they shouted at each other. It frightened him. He'd go and find somewhere safe to hide until they stopped, he decided. He headed a little farther down the path. His extending leash was quite long, so he could get a good distance away from the loud voices. The delicious smells in the undergrowth soon distracted him from the squabble he'd left behind, and he poked around the bushes, sure he could smell a rabbit somewhere nearby.

There was no rabbit to be found, but there was a huge butterfly, a brown one that swooped temptingly right in front of his nose. He barked happily and chased after it as it fluttered away. He'd never actually caught one before, but he was so close to this one, surely it couldn't get away this time. He ran on, barking excitedly and snapping at the butterfly, certain that Georgia and Adam would be pleased if he finally caught one.

Just then, Georgia grabbed at the leash, yanking it away from Adam. As she reached for its bulky plastic handle, she lost her balance and it slipped out of her hands. She dived after it, and so did Adam—but it was too late. They watched the leash slide away as Lucky raced after the butterfly.

"Lucky!" Georgia yelled, scrabbling after the leash as it disappeared down the path. She could just see Lucky's golden tail, wagging excitedly as he chased after something up ahead. Georgia set off to catch him—just as Lucky made one last desperate lunge after the butterfly and tumbled over the side of the cliff, his leash bouncing uselessly behind him.

# Chapter Six

Lucky scrabbled and scrambled down the steep slope, trying frantically to stop himself by clawing at the reddish side of the cliff as he fell. Sharper rocks stuck out of the sandy earth every so often, and he whimpered as one of his paws caught against a particularly large stone.

At last, he landed on a tiny ledge,

about five yards down the side of the cliff. He sat there cowering and shivering, holding up his bleeding paw and howling with fright. What had happened? All he had done was follow the butterfly! It had disappeared, and the path had gone with it. Where were Georgia and Adam? He wanted Georgia to take care of his paw and pet him, and get him out of this horrible place.

"Lucky!" Georgia screamed, as she raced along the path to the spot where he'd disappeared, with Adam dashing after her. "Where is he?" She flung herself down at the edge of the cliff to peer over, and felt suddenly sick, her head swimming as she looked at the ocean so far below. When they were on the beach, the cliffs had looked so pretty—pinkish red with sandy streaks. But now they seemed menacing and sinister, and very, very tall. The water came right up to the bottom now, foaming and rushing in with clouds of bubbles. Even though Lucky was a good swimmer, she didn't see how he could have survived such a terrible fall.

"Can you see him?" Adam asked, his voice quiet and miserable. Georgia shook her head. "No. He must be— under the water. . . ." she said, her voice choked with tears.

But then there was a pitiful wail from below, and Georgia gasped. "Adam, look! He's there, he's there!"

She pointed to a tiny ledge below, where a clump of bushes and straggly bits of grass had somehow managed to find some soil to grow in. It was just above the tumble of rocks rising out of the sea at the base of the cliff. Sitting there, staring up at them mournfully, was Lucky.

"Lucky, stay! We'll come and get you—or—or something. . . ." Georgia's voice trailed away.

"He's all right. He's actually okay!" Adam said, gripping tightly on to two handfuls of grass, and leaning as far as he possibly could without going over, too. "I can't believe he managed to fall down there and still be okay."

Georgia gulped, and tears welled up in her eyes. Adam put his arm around her. They were both shaking.

"He's moving, definitely. But I think he hurt his paw—it's so hard to see," Georgia murmured. "I shouldn't have tried to grab the leash from you. I'm really sorry." She stared down at Lucky. "How are we ever going to get him back? It's such a long way to that ledge."

Adam looked worriedly at Lucky. "I think you're right, he's holding his paw in a funny way. There's no way he'll be able to climb back up here! I wonder if I can scramble down to him."

Georgia grabbed his arm tightly. "Are you crazy? Look how steep it is! You'll fall!"

Adam shook his head. "Look. Just over there—it's almost like a path, down to where Lucky is."

"Well, I can't see it," Georgia said stubbornly. She sort of could, but it didn't look like much of a path, and she was scared that Adam was going to fall, too. It was just a very thin kind of ledge, weaving its way toward the bigger ledge that Lucky was on.

Lucky howled again, and Georgia called down to him. "It's okay, Lucky! Don't be scared!" She looked back up at Adam. "Are you sure you can get down there?"

Adam shrugged. "No. But I want to try. It was my fault that this happened, too." He went over to the little break in the cliff edge where the tiny path started, and stared at it, chewing his lip. "I'll sit and scoot down, I think." He edged himself down very slowly, and Georgia watched, her heart racing.

Lucky stared up from his ledge and wagged his tail hopefully. Adam was coming to get him! He stood up, wincing as he tried to put his hurt paw to the ground, and then he had to flop down again. There was definitely something wrong with his leg.

He could see Georgia, too, just her face, peering over the edge of the cliff, so very far away. Lucky let out a miserable howl. He wanted to be back up there with her!

"It's okay, Lucky—ssshhh!" Georgia called out, trying to make her voice calm and comforting. Their obedience class teacher had said that voices were really important. If she sounded frightened and upset, Lucky would be frightened, too. She had to keep him calm. He always listened best to her in obedience classes—Adam got him too excited. Now it was more important than ever before to keep Lucky calm. The little ledge he was on was so narrow. If Lucky got frightened and scrabbled around, he could so easily fall into the treacherous-looking water. And with an injured leg, he might not be able to swim.

Georgia watched nervously as Adam inched down the path toward Lucky. He was going as slowly and carefully as he could, but the path was very steep.

Suddenly, Georgia gasped as Adam's feet went out from under him, and he slid down in a rattle of sand and tiny pebbles. She caught her breath, jamming her knuckles into her mouth to stop herself from crying out.

Adam yelled in panic and grabbed hold of a bush, hanging on even though it scratched his hands.

"Adam!" Georgia called down. "Are you all right? You have to come back up—it isn't safe. We'll call Mom and Dad."

Adam nodded. "Sorry, Lucky," he called down sadly. "We're going to get help, I promise." He dragged himself back up, holding on to the scrubby plants that lined the path.

Georgia grabbed him as soon as he

got near the top. "We should have called Mom and Dad right away. Are you okay?"

Adam nodded. "Just a little scratched." He showed her his grazed hands. "But it was really scary. Poor Lucky. He fell a lot farther than I did." He reached into his pocket for the phone and pressed the Menu button to turn on the screen.

Nothing happened.

Georgia and Adam stared at it in horror. "Try again!" Georgia said hopefully, but the phone remained stubbornly lifeless.

"I must have hit it on something when I fell. Mom's going to be furious. . . ." Adam murmured.

"That doesn't matter now. What are we going to do?" Georgia looked around, hoping that there might be somebody else walking along the cliff top. But they were all alone.

"I'll have to run back down to the road—there's a pay phone, isn't there? I have some money left from yesterday. You stay here with Lucky. You can keep him calm, since you're good at that. We don't want him trying to climb up and falling even farther." Adam frowned. "Georgie, I can't remember Dad's cell phone number, can you?"

Georgia shook her head miserably. "No. But it doesn't matter," she added suddenly. "Dad wouldn't be able to get down the cliff, either. It's just too dangerous. You'll have to call the coast guard."

Adam nodded nervously. He'd never made an emergency call before—but this was definitely an emergency.

# Chapter Seven

Georgia watched as Adam raced off down the path, leaving her all alone on the cliff top, with only the seagulls shrieking around her. Then she leaned over the edge again, digging her toes into the sandy earth so that she felt safer wriggling a few inches farther out over the edge. She felt sick staring down at the water, which seemed to be crashing against the cliffs harder and harder every time she looked.

Lucky was curled up in a little ball now, with his nose tucked in next to his tail. He looked so tiny that Georgia wanted to cry.

"Lucky!" she called down to him.

Lucky glanced up and barked delightedly. He'd thought that Georgia and Adam had both gone and left him here. He had no idea how he was ever going to get back up the cliff. He'd looked down at the water on the rocks below him, and wondered if he should just jump in and swim till he found the beach, but the water looked very different from where he'd swam at the beach before. His little ledge was just above the waves, which kept rolling in and

98

sending cold spray up at him. And the rocks looked slippery and frightening. His paw hurt, too, and he wasn't sure he'd even be able to swim. He'd pressed himself back against the cliff wall instead and curled into a ball, whimpering sadly to himself, wishing someone was there to help him. And then he'd heard Georgia!

Could he climb back up to her? The ledge was very narrow, and it trailed away into a tiny little path that went winding up the cliff. Georgia wasn't really *that* far away, Lucky thought, staring up at her pale and anxious face. He limped along to where the ledge narrowed and looked thoughtfully up at the path. It was very narrow. He started to move up it, squeezing himself as close as he could to the side of the cliff and feeling the sand trickle down into his fur.

"Lucky, stay!" Georgia was calling to him. She sounded worried—angry, almost. He was only trying to get to her, so why was she angry? But he knew what "stay" meant from his obedience classes. He had to do as he was told, even though he really didn't want to. He sat down on the path, his ears drooping, feeling confused.

"It's okay, Lucky, sorry. I'm sorry." Up on the cliff, Georgia took a deep breath and tried not to feel afraid. It just felt like Adam had been gone for so long. Every time she looked down, Lucky's little ledge seemed to have grown even narrower, and the ocean wilder. And if the tide came up much more, the ledge would be underwater! She tried to remember when high tide had been the day before, but her mind felt foggy.

"Good boy, Lucky. Stay! What a good boy! Lots of treats soon. Stay! That's it." *Just don't move, Lucky, please!* she added silently to herself.

"Georgia! Georgia!"

Lucky looked up, his tail wagging. Adam had come back, too! He tried to bark happily to show Adam he was pleased to see him, but jumping around hurt his paw and his balance seemed all wrong. He slid backward, scrabbling and yelping, and Georgia's and Adam's faces appeared over the edge of the cliff, both looking horrified.

"Lucky, keep still!" Adam yelled. His voice was sharp and fierce, and it made Lucky scared. He skittered on the ledge anxiously.

"Down, Lucky! Down! Stay!" That was Georgia again. She didn't sound scared like Adam, but she sounded very firm. Not angry, but he could tell he had to do as she said or she would be. Lucky lay down flat on the ledge, feeling the cold water splash over his back. He wanted to get away. He hated it down here! He howled and howled. But he kept still.

Up above Lucky on the cliff, Adam explained to Georgia what was happening. "I got to the pay phone and called the coast guard. But I didn't know exactly where we were on the cliffs; I hope I told them the right place. I said it was near Cliff Cottage."

"Are they sending someone?" Georgia asked anxiously.

"Yes, they said the boat will come out from Woolbridge harbor, and it won't take long at all. The lady on the phone said it might even get here before I did."

"Did she say to do anything else?"

Adam shook his head. "Just to come back and try to keep Lucky calm, and you're doing that really well. And we should watch out for the boat and wave, in case they can't see Lucky." He propped himself up on his elbows, staring out to sea. "That's not a coast guard boat, is it?" he asked, pointing to a small boat far out on the waves.

Georgia shook her head. "No, I think that's the tour boat from Woolbridge. Anyway, I bet the coast guard boat won't be that far out. It'll come around the edge of the bay." She frowned down at Lucky on his ledge, and the nasty-looking rocks below him. "How are they going to get to him, Adam?

They won't be able to get a boat close up to those rocks, will they?"

"If it's an inflatable boat they will. I saw one in the boat shed when I went to Woolbridge Beach yesterday. It's made for going in and out of the rocks around the coast. Look, there are people on the cliffs—maybe they saw it being launched. Josh and Liam said people always go up there to watch when the coast guard boat goes out."

Georgia nodded, watching the little crowd of people gathering farther along the cliffs above the beach. She could see they were chatting and pointing at Lucky. If it had been another dog, she would have been interested, too. Now it only made her feel sick.

"Georgie, look! I can see it coming!"

The coast guard boat was roaring around the far edge of the cliffs in a cloud of spray, and bouncing over the water toward them. It was a small craft, and there were only three people on it, but it was very, very fast.

"I wish Mom and Dad were here," Georgia said worriedly as the little gray boat shot toward them. "Maybe they saw the boat being launched from Woolbridge when they were shopping. Do you think they'd come back to see what was going on?"

"Maybe. They might even be in that crowd over there." Adam hugged her.

The boat was getting closer now, and they could see the coastguardsmen waving to them. They waved back and pointed down to Lucky.

Lucky could see the boat coming, too. It was very loud, and he didn't like it at all. He barked at it, wishing it'd go away.

"Shhh, Lucky, it's okay!" Georgia called down. "I think he's scared of the boat. Lucky, stay!"

The coast guard boat had stopped by the rocks, and one of the men was climbing out. Georgia held her breath anxiously. It looked so slippery.

"Hello up there!" the man called to Adam and Georgia. "He looks pretty scared. Can you get him to stay? I don't want to frighten him into jumping."

Georgia nodded. "Lucky, stay there! Stay!"

Lucky stared wide-eyed at the man in the bright orange suit, with his huge life jacket and white helmet. He looked like some sort of strange creature, and he'd arrived in that large noisy thing that was still grumbling and snorting below him. Lucky gave a loud series of barks, trying to sound big and scary. But the man didn't go away. He climbed slowly closer instead. Lucky looked around, desperate for a way to escape. There was only the little narrow path where he'd already slipped. But he didn't have a choice. He started to back away up it, still barking at the strange man.

"Lucky, no!" It was Georgia, calling him from up above. "Stay! Lucky, stay!"

Lucky knew he should do as he was told, but he didn't want to stay! The strange man was coming after him!

"Stay, Lucky!" It was Georgia's firmest voice. If he did as he was told, he might get dog treats—he knew Georgia had them in her bag. And he was very hungry. The man was coming closer. Lucky stayed still and looked imploringly up at Georgia. Did he really have to stay?

"Yes, good boy, Lucky! Stay!" Georgia sounded pleased with him.

The man was almost at his ledge now, and Lucky wanted to growl at him. He didn't look nice at all with that big white helmet on. But he kept quiet. He was sure Georgia would want him to.

"You're a good dog, aren't you?" the man called as he climbed onto the ledge. The man's voice was actually quite nice, and Lucky stopped shivering. "Look what I've got." The coastguardsman held out a bit of a treat, and Lucky gulped it down gratefully. Maybe the man wasn't so bad after all, even if he did look scary. "Want some more treats?" The man reached down and picked up Lucky, and gave him a whole treat this time. "Aren't you a little star? Let's go down." And he started back over the rocks to the boat, with Lucky tucked tightly under one arm.

Up on the top of the cliff, Georgia hugged Adam tightly. "They've got him! They've got him! Lucky's really going to be okay!"

# Chapter Eight

Adam hugged Georgia back, laughing, and then turned back to peer over the edge. "Hey, shhh, they're calling us!"

"We'll take him around to the small beach in the boat!" one of the men shouted up to Adam and Georgia. "We'll meet you there, okay? You're both all right, aren't you? Not hurt at all?"

"We're fine! Thank you!" Adam yelled back, and Georgia called, "Good boy, Lucky!" They raced back along the top of the cliff as fast as they could, heading for the path down to the beach right in front of the cottage.

"I can see our car parked behind the cottage!" Adam yelled to Georgia. "Mom and Dad are probably down on the beach. We would've met them on the path if they'd come after us—they must have seen the boat and gone to watch."

They scrambled down the path and ran across the sand to the little group of people who'd gathered to watch the coast guard boat pull in. It beached with a soft crunch of sand, and one of the men jumped over the side into the water, which only came halfway up his big orange boots. Another of the coastguardsmen handed Lucky over the side to the man, and Georgia ran into the water to take him, even though she had her sneakers on.

Lucky was squeaking with delight at seeing Georgia and Adam, and he wriggled wildly, trying to get out of the man's arms to reach her.

"He's a lovely little dog, isn't he?" the man told her as he handed Lucky over. "Did I hear you calling him Lucky?"

Georgia nodded, and the man laughed. "Well, you certainly named him right. He's very lucky. Could have been a lot worse. You look after him, now. Don't let him go near the edge of any more cliffs."

"I won't," Georgia said. "It was my fault he fell. We'll be more careful, I promise." She laughed as Lucky licked her all over, and then licked Adam's face, too.

"You were right to call 9-1-1, though," the man told them. "Don't you ever go climbing down those cliffs yourselves."

Adam shuddered. "We won't."

"Georgia! Adam!"

Mom and Dad were making their way through the small crowd, looking horrified.

"What on earth happened?" Mom demanded.

"Sorry, Mom. . . ." they murmured. "There was an accident," Georgia added. "Lucky went over the edge of the cliff."

"That cliff?" Dad gazed up at it, his face pale. "But we agreed you'd keep him on the leash up there." Dad looked from Georgia to Adam. He seemed really disappointed.

"They did the right thing," the coastguardsman told Mom and Dad. "They called 9-1-1, and got us out to help."

Mom nodded. "Thank you so much."

Georgia caught her arm. "Mom, can we explain later, please? Lucky hurt his leg when he fell, and we have to take him to a vet."

"There's a vet on Main Street in Woolbridge, right by the supermarket," the coastguardsman told them. "Good luck. I hope it's nothing too serious." And he splashed back to the boat, with everyone waving and cheering as they sped away.

Lucky yawned sleepily and licked at the bandage on his paw. It was itchy, and he was sure if he nibbled it carefully he could pull it off.

"Hey, don't do that, Lucky." Georgia sat down beside him and tickled him under the chin. "You know if you keep chewing it, you'll have to wear that horrible collar thing, and you wouldn't like that. The vet says the bandage has to stay on for at least a week."

"He was so lucky not to break anything," Mom said. "You really did choose the right name, Georgia. Only four stitches, and some pulled muscles. It could have been so much worse." Mom's face was serious. After they'd gotten back from the vet's the day before, she and Dad had made Georgia and Adam sit down and tell them exactly what had happened up on the cliff path. The children felt awful as they explained that it was all their fault that Lucky fell and got hurt. Then Mom and Dad had told them how disappointed they were.

Georgia shivered. "I know," she said. "I don't want to go along the cliff-top path ever again."

"Me, neither," Adam agreed, munching on chocolate-spread toast.

"It's a pity not to go out, though," said Mom, getting up to check the weather from the window. "It's such a beautiful day. You two could go down to the beach with Dad, if you like. I can stay and watch Lucky."

Georgia shook her head, and glanced at Adam to see that he was doing the same. "I'd rather stay here and be with Lucky," she explained. "Yesterday was so scary. I just want to be with him for a while." She petted his ears lovingly, and Lucky yawned and nudged her with his little damp nose.

Adam came over and slipped Lucky a dog treat. Lucky gulped it down happily. Everyone was being so nice to him!

Dad nodded. "Well, we've still got three more days left here. Lucky might be all right to go down to the beach tomorrow if we're careful. And it's good just having a quiet day, anyway."

There was a loud knock at the door, and Adam burst out laughing.

Dad sighed. "What did I say that for?" He got up and went to the front door, coming back with a dark-haired woman who had a big camera hanging around her neck. "It seems you two are famous," Dad said, smiling. "This is Melissa, from the local paper. She heard all about yesterday's adventure, and wants a photo of you and Lucky."

"It's such a lovely story," the reporter explained. "And apparently you called the coast guard yourselves? That was really good thinking."

Adam grinned proudly. "That was me. But it was actually Georgia who kept Lucky safe the whole time he was on the ledge. She was amazing at getting him to stay."

Georgia smiled. "But it was our fault Lucky fell," she added sadly. "We were arguing over who got to hold his leash and then we dropped it, and he ran off and slipped over the cliff edge."

Melissa smiled. "I don't think I'll put that in. These things happen, don't they? I used to fight with my brother all the time. We'll just remind people to be extra careful when they're walking up on the cliffs." Lucky jumped down from the sofa and went to give her a curious sniff. "And this is Lucky?" She patted Lucky, and he licked her fingers, making her laugh. "He's a real sweetheart. And it sounds like he really was lucky!"

Lucky heard his name and barked happily. The lady was right, he was Lucky, he knew that!

Georgia beamed as they posed with Lucky for the newspaper photo—she and Adam on either side of their beautiful puppy. She knew he'd had an amazing escape. Georgia petted Lucky's silky golden ears and smiled at the camera.

Just now, she felt like the luckiest girl ever.

# Also
# Available:

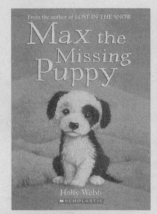

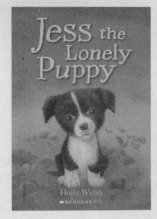

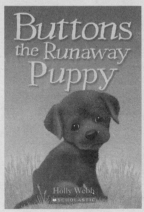

Lost in the Storm

Holly Webb
SCHOLASTIC

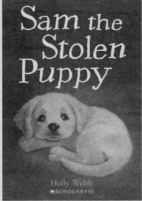

Sam the Stolen Puppy

Holly Webb
SCHOLASTIC

Alfie all Alone

Holly Webb
SCHOLASTIC

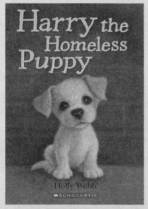

Harry the Homeless Puppy

Holly Webb
SCHOLASTIC

Timmy in Trouble

Holly Webb
SCHOLASTIC

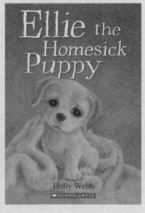

Ellie the Homesick Puppy

Holly Webb
SCHOLASTIC

Alone in the Night

Holly Webb
SCHOLASTIC

Misty the Abandoned Kitten

Holly Webb
SCHOLASTIC

# My Naughty Little Puppy

Holly Webb

When Ellie names her puppy Rascal, she doesn't realize how right she is! The playful little puppy is soon getting himself and Ellie into all sorts of mischief. . . .

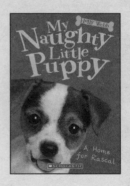